For Luke,
and
Archie and Max

First U.S. edition 1990

Library of Congress Cataloging-in-Publication Data

Clark, Emma Chichester.
Catch that hat!/Emma Chichester Clark.
p.   cm.
Summary: When the wind blows away her favorite hat,
Rose, her friend Archie, and an assortment of animals
chase the elusive hat all over the countryside.
ISBN 0–316–14496–7
[1. Hats — Fiction.   2. Stories in rhyme.]   I. Title.
PZ8.3.C5395Cat   1990
[E] — dc20   89–34881
                                          CIP
                                          AC

10 9 8 7 6 5 4 3 2 1
First published in Great Britain in 1988
by The Bodley Head, London

Printed in Italy

CATCH THAT HAT!

Emma Chichester Clark

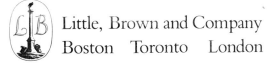

Little, Brown and Company
Boston   Toronto   London

One day Rose was chasing a cat
When the wind blew away her favorite hat.
"Oh, no!" said Rose. "Drat that cat!
I can't just lose my hat like that."

The hat landed on the roof next door.
Rose couldn't reach it, she was sure.

Archie climbed up and threw it out,
But the wind was strong, the hat blew about.

It whooshed away up in the sky,
Over some trees and a pig in his sty.
It stopped on a steep hill far away.
"Oh, no," said Rose, "it's not my day!"

Jack had seen it
sailing past,

So he raced up the hill
extremely fast.

He rescued the hat
and put it on.

But seconds later
it was gone.

It flew in the air, back into the sky,
Then into a lake; Rose let out a cry,
"Oh, my hat, my hat, my favorite hat!
Gone with the wind. Oh, dear! Oh, drat!"

They all got into Flora's boat.
It had a leak but stayed afloat.
Jack caught the hat in Flora's net.
It was shiny and slimy and terribly wet.

But as Jack gave it back to Rose,
He had a tickle in his nose.
He sneezed the most enormous sneeze.
The hat went flying in the breeze.

It flew away faster than ever.
"Oh, Jack," said Rose,
"that wasn't clever."

The hat flew over trees and people,
Then it landed on a steeple.
"Oh, my," said Rose.
"It's gone so high!"
"Nonsense," said George.
"Just watch me fly!"

He flew to the steeple and snatched up that hat,
But then he saw Nora the tortoiseshell cat.

He shouted, "Hello" and "How do you do?"
As he opened his beak, away the hat flew.
"Oh, drat!" said Rose. "That hat's in a spin."
The hat reached a cave; the hat flew in.

Nora followed with Alice and Joe.
It was awfully dark, so Rose didn't go.

Joe carried the hat, he was shaking with fright.
Rose shouted, "Make sure you hold on tight."
Joe tried to hold on, but her voice made him jump.
And the hat sailed away as he fell with a bump.

It got all tangled up
in a strange tall tree.

Rose said,
"Drat! that hat is
annoying me.
It's driving me crazy
but even so,
I still can't bear
to let it go."

Rose, Archie, Jack, George and Flora
Stood with Alice, Joe and Nora
Thinking of ways to get it down.
"No way," said Edward. He made a frown.

"Because it's a Monkey Puzzle tree,
And no one could climb it, not even me."

"What a waste," said Rose. She started to cry.
"No, it isn't," said Nancy, flying by.
"It's a wonderful nest, the best I've known.
And if you don't mind I'll make it my own."

She filled it with leaves and made it trim
And soon they saw little ones over the brim.
What a lovely hat to live in,
thought Rose.
A tear went trickling
down her nose.

Edward and Nancy and Archie and Flora
Jack, Alice and Joe, George and Nora
Gave Rose a great big box with a bow.
Oh, what is inside? I think I know.

It's a beautiful hat, a hat that won't go
Rushing off when the wind starts to blow.
There's a ribbon to fasten it under her chin . . .

And when it is windy, Rose will stay in.